REX JONES

SAFECRACKERS

BY JONNY ZUCKER

ILLUSTRATED BY ENZO TROIANO
COVER ILLUSTRATION BY MARCUS SMITH

Librarian Reviewer
Marci Peschke
Librarian, Dallas Independent School District
MA Education Reading Specialist, Stephen F. Austin State University
Learning Resources Endorsement, Texas Women's University

Reading Consultant
Mary Evenson
Middle School Teacher, Edina Public Schools, MN
MA in Education, University of Minnesota

STONE ARCH BOOKS
Minneapolis   San Diego

First published in the United States in 2007
by Stone Arch Books,
151 Good Counsel Drive, P.O. Box 669,
Mankato, Minnesota 56002.
www.stonearchbooks.com

Originally published in Great Britain in 2005
by Badger Publishing Ltd.

Library of Congress Cataloging-in-Publication Data
Zucker, Jonny.
   [Cash Snatch]
   Safecrackers / by Jonny Zucker; illustrated by Enzo Troiano.
   p. cm. — (Keystone Books (Rex Jones))
   Originally published: Great Britain: Badger Publishing Ltd., 2005,
under the title The Cash Snatch.
   Summary: When fifteen-year-old Rex Jones's mysterious cell phone
transports him and his friends, Dave and Carl, into a bank's high-
powered security center, the three are charged with preventing notorious
bank robber Razor Bell from breaking into the vault.
   ISBN-13: 978-1-59889-331-1 (library binding)
   ISBN-10: 1-59889-331-9 (library binding)
   ISBN-13: 978-1-59889-427-1 (paperback)
   ISBN-10: 1-59889-427-7 (paperback)
   [1. Adventure and adventurers—Fiction. 2. Bank robberies—
Fiction. 3. Security guards—Fiction. 4. Cellular telephones—Fiction.]
I. Troiano, Enzo, ill. II. Title.
PZ7.Z77925Saf 2007
[Fic]—dc22   2006026733

1 2 3 4 5 6 12 11 10 09 08 07

Printed in the United States of America

TABLE OF CONTENTS

How It All Began

Fifteen-year-old Rex Jones used to have a pretty normal life. He went to school. He hung out with his best friends, Carl and Dave. He played sports. He watched TV. Normal stuff.

Then, a few months ago, Rex bought a new cell phone. It was the last one the store had. Rex had seen the phone in a magazine, but his new phone was different in one way.

It had two extra buttons. One said EXPLORE and one said RETURN. The man in the store said that none of the other phones had those buttons.

The phone worked fine at first. Rex forgot about the extra buttons.

One day the phone started to make a strange buzzing sound. When Rex looked at it, the green EXPLORE button was flashing.

He pressed it, and suddenly found himself in an incredible dream world of adventures. Each adventure could only be ended when Rex's phone buzzed again and the flashing red RETURN button was pressed.

He never knows when an adventure will begin, and he never knows if it will end in time to save him.

CHAPTER 1
SECURITY

One boring day, when nothing much was happening, Rex Jones and his best friends, Carl and Dave, were in the candy store. Dave picked up a chocolate bar and a pack of gum.

"That's a dollar," said the cashier.

Dave looked in his wallet. He only had 75 cents.

"Um, sorry," he said. "I don't have enough money."

At that very second, Rex felt a buzzing. He looked at his cell phone. The green EXPLORE button was flashing.

He looked at his friends. They nodded. Rex pressed the button.

There was a flash of white light. The next thing they knew, the boys were standing on a platform looking out over a very busy room. People were making phone calls, working at computer screens, and talking to customers.

A large man with green eyes, wearing a striped suit, walked over to them. "Welcome to the National Bank," he said. "I am Mr. Todd. I'm in charge of the bank's security. Below you is the bank floor."

"Why are we here?" asked Dave.

"The last security guards didn't do their job well enough, so I asked for some younger ones. I have to admit, I didn't mean quite so young, but I suppose you'll be fine."

"What do you mean?" asked Rex.

"There are rumors that Razor Bell, the most wanted bank robber in the country, is going to try the crime of the century sometime very soon," said Mr. Todd. "Our security system is the best in the world, but he's the smartest crook there is."

"And?" asked Carl.

"And," Mr. Todd replied, "I have to be out of the country for the next twenty-four hours. So you three will be in charge of the bank's security."

CHAPTER 2
THE MAIN VAULT

Before he left, Mr. Todd took the three boys on a tour of the bank. Then he showed them the huge security room. There were twenty television screens, showing every room of the bank.

"These screens must be watched the whole time," said Mr. Todd. "I suggest that one of you stays in here, while the other two walk around the bank. Take turns so you stay alert."

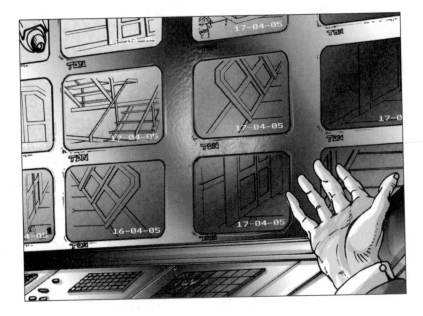

Then Mr. Todd took them deep underground in an elevator. They walked along a white hallway and stopped in front of a huge red door with a window panel in its center.

"This," said Mr. Todd, "is the bank's main vault. The door and its window are bulletproof and bombproof. Inside, we are storing more than a hundred million dollars."

He paused, then continued in a very serious voice. "You must guard it with your lives. Do you understand?"

Rex, Carl, and Dave nodded.

Mr. Todd pulled a plastic card from his pocket and handed it to Rex.

"This is the only key to the main vault," said Mr. Todd. "It can open and close the vault door from the inside and the outside."

He looked at Rex. "You will be in charge of this key while I'm away."

Rex slipped the plastic card into his jacket pocket.

CHAPTER 3
RAZOR BELL

Mr. Todd sat the boys down in front of a computer screen. They watched as a man's face appeared on the screen.

"That," said Mr Todd, "is Razor Bell. This photo is ten years old and he is a master of disguise. The only thing that never changes is that x-shaped scar above his left eye." He checked his watch. "I have to leave now," said Mr Todd. "See you in twenty-four hours."

The first twenty-three hours were very quiet. Rex, Carl, and Dave took turns watching the security screens and patrolling the bank.

Halfway through their last hour on duty, Rex and Carl were checking out the building, while Dave watched the security screens. Suddenly Rex and Carl heard the sound of screaming from the bank floor.

They ran to the main floor.

In the far corner of the bank floor, there was a cloud of smoke rising from flames. People were yelling and running for cover.

"It's a bomb!" someone screamed.

Rex and Carl froze. A man with a freckled face and a tall woman crashed into them, and they all fell to the floor.

Rex and Carl quickly stood up. The smoke and flames had vanished. Rex picked up a partly burned firecracker and a box of matches. He put the matches into his pocket.

"Everything is okay!" he called out to the bank's workers. "It must have been some kids messing around."

The screaming stopped, and slowly, everyone went back to work.

CHAPTER 4
THE SWITCH

Rex and Carl went back to the security room. Dave was sitting with his feet on a desk eating popcorn.

"Good work with that fire," Dave said. "I watched it from here."

"Did you see anything else?" Carl asked.

"Nothing," replied Dave. "I just talked to some guy who is interested in security and stuff. That was cool."

"You left this room?" asked Rex.

"It was only for five minutes," Dave replied.

"What did this man look like?" asked Rex.

"He was a big guy with a freckled face," replied Dave. "Why?"

Rex thought back to the freckled guy and the tall woman that he and Carl had bumped into. He quickly reached inside his jacket pocket for the main vault key card.

It was gone.

"Look at security screen seventeen," whispered Carl suddenly.

Screen seventeen showed the inside of the main vault.

Every other screen showed today's date and the time. But screen seventeen showed yesterday's date.

Rex was already halfway out of the room. "They switched the security tapes when Dave was in the hallway," he yelled. "This tape doesn't show what's happening now. The crooks are in there! Come on!"

CHAPTER 5
BREAK IN

The three reached the main vault. The door was wide open. The people who had bumped into Rex and Carl were inside, taking money from giant steel boxes and putting it into mailbags.

A wig and some women's clothes were on the floor.

The woman was a man.

The other guy didn't have freckles any more. He'd been wearing some sort of mask.

The boys could now see the x-shaped scar above his left eye.

Both of the people had put on mailman uniforms.

"It's Razor Bell," Rex whispered.

Razor spun around and saw them.

"You three get in here now," he shouted, waving a fist at them. "Sit on the floor over there and keep your mouths shut."

Rex, Carl, and Dave did as he said.

"In a couple of minutes we'll be out of here," said Razor with an evil laugh. "And the only thing people will see is two mailmen with sacks of letters."

CHAPTER 6
FIREWORKS

Rex, Carl, and Dave sat on the floor and watched the men stuff more cash into the sacks. The boys didn't know what to do next.

Suddenly Rex had an idea.

He reached into his pocket. He had the box of matches, a candy bar wrapper, and a crumpled paper bag from his lunch the day before. He tossed the wrapper aside.

Then he slipped his hands behind his back and set the bag on fire.

He tossed it through the vault's open door, and it landed in a wastebasket in the hallway, just underneath the smoke detector. The fire alarm started to howl.

"What's that?" shouted Razor.

The second man ran into the corridor to investigate. Razor followed.

As Razor ran out, Rex snatched something from Razor's pocket. Razor didn't notice.

As soon as the men were both outside, Rex pulled the vault door shut and swiped the plastic card key he'd taken from Razor's pocket.

The vault door locked, clicking into place. Then Rex pressed the black alarm button on the wall. More alarms started ringing all over the building.

Razor and the other man looked up. Through the vault door's window, they could see Rex, Carl, and Dave laughing at them. The crooks banged angrily on the door.

Just then, a team of police officers stormed down the corridor. The two crooks held up their hands and were taken away.

Rex turned the alarm off. For a few minutes, it was quiet in the vault. "Look at all this money," said Dave, pulling some bills from one of the sacks. "It could get us football season tickets for the rest of our lives!"

"We could each buy a house," said
Carl, grinning.

"I'm going to keep some," said
Dave, picking up a bunch of ten-dollar
bills from one of the sacks.

"Put that down!" said Rex.

A face appeared at the vault's
window. It was Mr. Todd. Rex swiped the
plastic card and the vault door opened.

CHAPTER 7
CASHING IN

Half an hour later, Rex, Carl, and Dave were standing with Mr. Todd on the platform overlooking the bank floor. Everyone on the bank floor was looking up at them.

"These three young men have just stopped Razor Bell from stealing a hundred million dollars from us!" Mr. Todd announced. Everyone below them began to clap and cheer.

Mr. Todd shook Rex and Carl's hands. But when Dave pulled out his hand to shake Mr. Todd's hand, a large bunch of ten-dollar bills fell out of his pocket onto the floor.

"Dave!" shouted Rex. "I told you not to take any!"

"Um, I'm sorry," said Dave. His face was red.

There were gasps from below. "You tricked me!" yelled Mr. Todd.

"No!" shouted Dave. "I was only joking. Really. Here, take it back!"

It was too late. Mr. Todd pressed an alarm button and lots of police officers appeared again.

"Run!" yelled Rex.

The boys raced down the hallway. Mr. Todd and the police were right behind them.

At the end of the hallway, there were five different ways to go. "Which way?" screamed Carl.

Just then, Rex's phone buzzed and the red RETURN button flashed. He quickly pressed it.

Suddenly the boys were back in the candy store. "So, do you have enough money, or what?" said the cashier, looking bored.

Dave searched through his pockets, hoping to find a ten-dollar bill. "Um, I guess not," he replied.

Rex smiled. "Not anymore, anyway!" he said.

About the Author

Even as a child, Jonny Zucker wanted to be a writer. Today, he has written more than 30 books. He has also spent time working as a teacher, song writer, and stand-up comedian. Jonny lives in London with his wife and two children.

About Marcus Smith

Marcus Smith says that he started drawing when his mother put a pen in his hand when he was a baby. Smith grew up in Chicago, where he took classes at the world famous Art Institute. In Chicago he also designed band logos and tattoos! He moved west and studied at the Minneapolis College of Art and Design, majoring in both Illustration and Comic Art. As an artist, Smith was "influenced by the land of superheroes, fantasy, horror, and action," and he continues to work in the world of comics.

GLOSSARY

bombproof (BOM-proof)—made to protect people from the blast of a bomb

bulletproof (BUL-uht-proof)—made to protect people from bullets

cashier (ka-SHEER)—someone who takes in or gives out money, in a bank or store

fate (FAYT)—what will happen to someone

panel (PAN-uhl)—a flat piece of material made to form part of a wall or door

rumor (ROO-mur)—something said by many people; often untrue

security (si-KYOOR-it-ee)—safety; also, the people who maintain safety

vault (VAWLT)—a room or compartment used for keeping money and valuables safe

wanted (WONT-id)—someone the police are looking for

DISCUSSION QUESTIONS

1. What was the biggest mistake the boys made while they were guarding the bank? What would you have done differently?

2. At the end of the book, Dave thinks he might still have some of the bank's money in his pockets. If he had, would it have been wrong for him to buy candy with the money? Why, or why not?

3. Do you think it was right for Dave to take some of the money? Do you think he was telling the truth when he said that it was just a joke and he was going to give it back? Why, or why not?

WRITING PROMPTS

1. Have you ever been put in charge of taking care of something important? What was it? Who put you in charge of it? What happened? Write about it.

2. Rex doesn't know where his phone will send him next. If you could pick a place to be sent, where would it be? What would you do there? Who would you want to take with you?

ALSO BY
JONNY ZUCKER

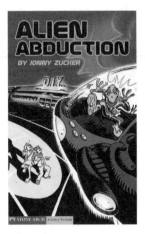

Alien Abduction

When Shelly and Dan are abducted by Zot the alien, they teach him about the ways of earthling teenagers. Hopefully they can convince Mr. Tann of their story before they end up in big trouble!

Summer Trouble

Tom's summer plans change when his cousin Ben decides to visit. Tom believes his entire vacation will be ruined, until Ben comes to his rescue in a tight situation.

MORE REX JONES ADVENTURES

Inside the Game

Rex Jones's extraordinary cell phone transports him and his friends, Carl and Dave, inside the action of a new videogame. Will they master the race cars of the Chase of Death, or will they crash and burn?

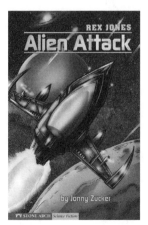

Alien Attack

Rex Jones's cell phone transports him and his friends to a space ship high above Earth. A battle is about to begin, and Rex, Carl, and Dave have to save the planet — if they can!

INTERNET SITES

Do you want to know more about subjects related to this book? Or are you interested in learning about other topics? Then check out FactHound, a fun, easy way to find Internet sites.

Our investigative staff has already sniffed out great sites for you!

Here's how to use FactHound:

1. Visit *www.facthound.com*

2. Select your grade level.

3. To learn more about subjects related to this book, type in the book's ISBN number: **1598893319**.

4. Click the **Fetch It** button.

FactHound will fetch the best Internet sites for you!